This book belongs to:

FiNIeY

To Claudine for the pink. To Mom for life. To my Sun and all my umbrellas . . . And to Eliott, in all weather! — A.C.

To my pink candy goddesses: Marguerite and Selma. — G.G.

"The rain falls as we fall in love,
cheering the forecasts."
— Martin Page

Tundra Books, an imprint of Penguin Random House Canada Young Readers,
a Penguin Random House Company

Library and Archives Canada Cataloguing in Publication

Callot, Amélie, 1981-
[Rose à petits pois. English]
      The pink umbrella / Amélie Callot ; illustrator, Geneviève Godbout.

Translation of: Rose à petits pois.
Issued in print and electronic formats.
ISBN 978-1-101-91923-1 (hardcover).— ISBN 978-1-101-91924-8 (EPUB)

I. Godbout, Geneviève, 1985-, illustrator II. Title.
III. Title: Rose à petits pois. English

PZ7.1.C35Pi 2018   j843'.92   C2017-900557-X
                                            C2017-900558-8

Published simultaneously in the United States of America by Tundra Books of Northern New York, an imprint of Penguin Random House Canada Young Readers, a Penguin Random House Company

Originally published in French in 2016 by Les Éditions de la Pastèque, Montreal, Quebec, Canada

Library of Congress Control Number: 2017931044

English edition edited by Tara Walker and Jessica Burgess
Translated by Lara Hinchberger
Designed by Stéphane Ulrich
The artwork in this book was rendered in pastels and colored pencils.
The text was handlettered by Geneviève Godbout.

Printed and bound in China

www.penguinrandomhouse.ca

1 2 3 4 5   22 21 20 19 18

The Pink Umbrella

words by **Amélie Callot**

pictures by **Geneviève Godbout**

tundra

"One rose, one daisy, one tulip.
One rose, one daisy, one tulip."

Adele makes bouquets with flowers that Lucas, the grocer from the nearest town, brings her. She places them on the tables of her café, The Polka-Dot Apron.

The bouquets are pretty and they smell nice.

Lucas brings Adele flowers twice a week. On Wednesdays, he sets up a stall with fresh fruits and vegetables in the café so the villagers can restock their pantries.

On Sundays, he comes just so that Adele can make her new bouquets.

Lucas is very reliable, and he always takes off his cap when he comes into the café.

"One rose, one daisy, one tulip. Perfect!"
Adele is satisfied.

She smooths the apron she wears every day
and tucks a rosebud into her upswept hair.

These little details make her regular customers
love coming to The Polka-Dot Apron.

And Adele loves her regulars.

The Polka-Dot Apron is not just a café. On Wednesdays,
it's also a market. On Saturdays, it's also a cinema. Sometimes
during the week, there are parties in the evenings. On Sundays,
it's closed. That is, it's open only to regulars.

But nearly everyone who comes to the café is a regular, and the door is never closed to strangers, so it's really open every day of the year!

The café stands in the midst of a small group of houses that face into the wind, looking out at the ocean. The coast is rugged, but the land is gentle, covered in tall grasses blown flat by the sea air.

Aside from the residents of the village, there is very little here in this wild landscape.

For the villagers, the café is a refuge,
a small lantern always lit.

It's where everyone meets. Where they cry, laugh, yell, argue and love. The café is the heart of the village.

And Adele is the heart of the café. She is the village's sun — lively, sweet and sparkling.

She is known for gathering people together. And whenever she closes the shop to go down to the beach or to take a walk, she always finds a customer waiting patiently for her to return.

She finally asked Lucas to make her a bench to set in front of the café, for the regulars.

Lucas can do a little bit of everything and can do it well.

And he looks out for Adele.

The thing everyone knows about Adele is that she doesn't like the rain.

When the weather is nice, she smiles, she whistles, she sings at the top of her lungs, she throws open the windows and props open the door.

Sometimes, she leaves the café for an hour of freedom. She doesn't stay away long, but still, she loves the sunshine!

But when it rains, Adele stays inside.
She can't help it; she loses her spirit.
The rain is gray, cold and dreary.

Fewer regulars make the trip to the café to say hello.
And what's more, the rain dirties up her floors!

You can say anything, argue as hard as you can, but it won't make a bit of difference. Adele will not stick even the tip of her nose outside.

Sometimes, she shuts down the café, rolls up in her quilt and waits for the sun to take the place of the clouds.

One sunny Wednesday, a market day, there was a crowd in the café.
Customers pressed together; they jostled, they huddled, they swarmed.
This one asked for orange juice, that one asked for a melon . . .

Adele was in heaven! She adores the mood on market day.
She asked for news from the smallest child and from
Great-Aunt Aimee. She never forgets anyone.

At closing time, Adele took off her shoes to sweep and clean her café. (There wasn't much to do, as Lucas never leaves without helping out and putting all the furniture back where it belongs.)

That was when she found, under the coatrack, a pair of boots!

Who would have worn boots on such a beautiful day? And left without them? They were such pretty pink rubber boots.

The owner must have had small feet, since they fit Adele.

She looked at them from every angle and discovered a sun carved in each sole.

"Well," she said to herself, "at least it won't be difficult to find out who owns a pair of small pink boots with suns carved in the soles. But for tonight, I'll just set them behind the counter."

For the rest of the week, Adele asked her customers, but none of them had lost their boots. And no one could guess who the pretty pink boots belonged to . . .

"Except maybe to Adele!" suggested Emma the dressmaker to Thomas the mechanic over a cup of steaming tea.

(Emma also loves pink, but she has big feet.)

Wednesday came again, as sunny and warm as the week
before. Lucas returned as well, to set up his stall.

And, of course, customers rushed to get in line.

Adele had not thought of the mystery boots all day —
she was too busy to slow down!

But that evening, at closing time, she found a pink
raincoat hanging on the coatrack at the entrance.

"Well, that's strange!" Adele said as she touched the coat.

She was certain she hadn't seen anyone with it. And who
would have worn a raincoat on such a warm day?

She took the raincoat off the rack, studied it more closely and slipped it on. An exact fit. Adele thought it was very well made, and it looked nice too.

"And with the belt, it really is perfect," she said to herself, looking in the mirror.

Adele didn't stop wondering about the boots and coat. She examined the mystery from all sides and could see only one solution: this time, she was sure it couldn't have been an accident. If the boots and coat fit her so well, it was because they were meant for her!

Adele didn't mention her discovery, but the next Wednesday, she didn't take her eyes off the coatrack.

It wasn't hard, as the weather was bad and there were few customers.

In the middle of the afternoon, Lucas announced
that he was going to take down his stall early.
The rain hadn't stopped falling, and practically
no one had shown up all day.

Adele was gloomy — nothing would happen today.
Nothing ever happened on gray days.

So she helped Lucas pack up his fruit and vegetables. Then the grocer got into his truck, and she waved to him from the doorway so she wouldn't get wet.

When the truck disappeared from view, Adele turned around to close the café, roll herself up in her quilt and wait for the sun to take the place of the clouds . . .

But she stopped short, stunned! In the entrance,
under the coatrack, was an adorable umbrella.
It was pink . . . with polka dots!

And only one person could have left it there.

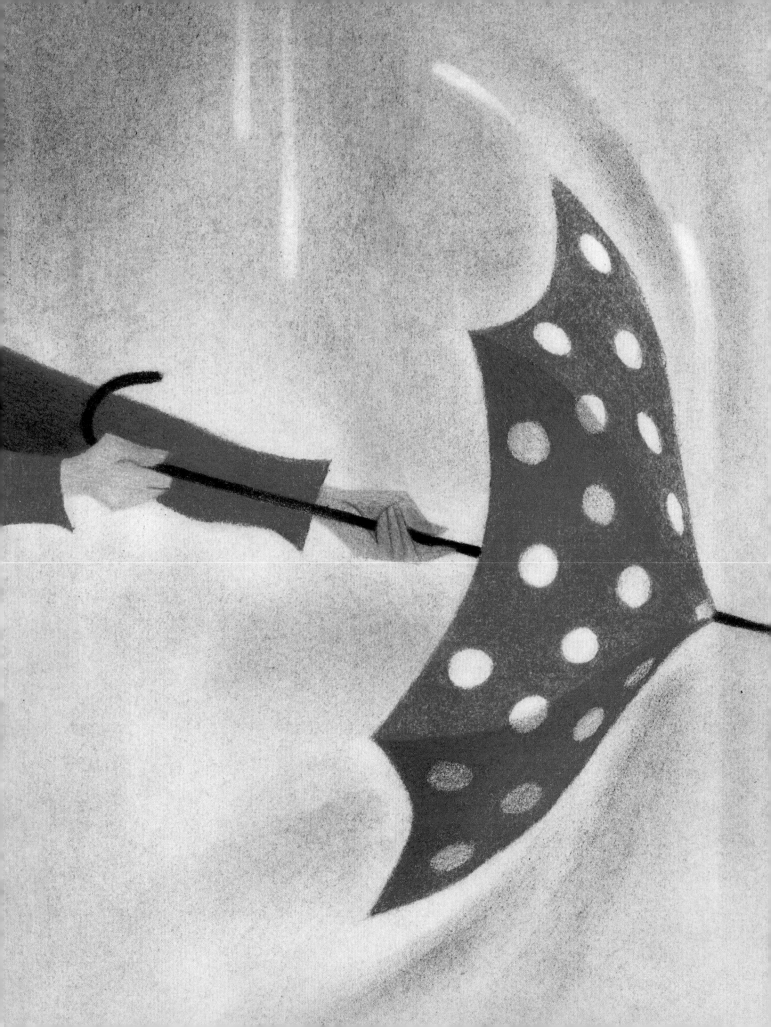

Adele smiled.

Because the day was done, because she
wanted to, and because opening an umbrella
inside is bad luck . . . Adele put on the boots
and the raincoat and, on the doorstep, opened
the pink polka-dotted umbrella.

There was only one step to take, and she
took it with joy. She turned the key in the
lock and went for a walk in the rain.

It really wasn't so bad. The air smelled wonderfully of damp grass, and the rain played a pretty melody as it fell on the umbrella.

The wind was fresh, the drops slid
off the leaves, the snails were out.

Adele followed her own path, her boots in the mud,
her nose in the flowers and a smile on her lips.

And there, beside the road, she saw Lucas's truck . . .

Adele found Lucas totally soaked! His truck was stuck in the mud.

Lucas shrugged. "I can't get out. I'll have to wait for the rain to stop," he said, discouraged. With a small smile, he added, "You have a pretty umbrella."

Adele blushed.

"Why not come and wait in the café? We'll have to walk, but there's room for two under the umbrella."

And so they went.

On the way, the storm ended. But neither of the two friends seemed to notice. They were so happy, walking close together under the umbrella to keep dry . . .

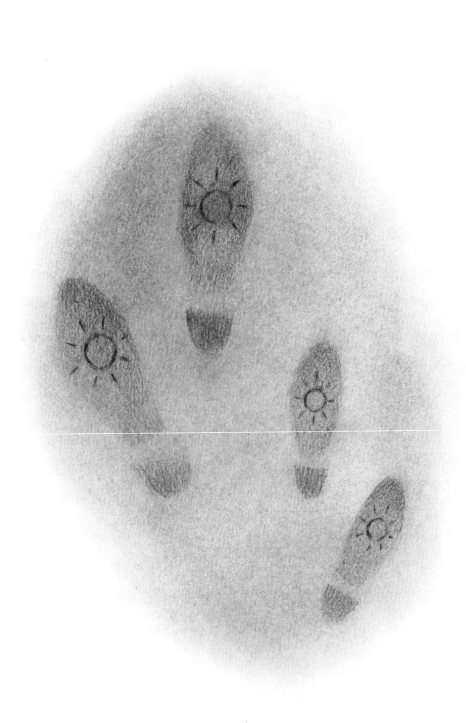

. . . they didn't see that their footsteps left four small shining suns in the soft, wet ground.